KINDRED SPIRITS

Rainbow Rowell lives in Omaha, Nebraska, with her husband and two sons.

She's also the author of *Attachments*, *Eleanor & Park*, *Fangirl*, *Landline* and *Carry On*.

Visit her website at www.rainbowrowell.com.

KINDRED SPIRITS

FROM THE BESTSELLING AUTHOR OF *FANGIRL*

RAINBOW ROWELL

FOR OLDER READERS

MACMILLAN

First published 2016 by Macmillan Children's Books
an imprint of Pan Macmillan
20 New Wharf Road, London N1 9RR
Associated companies throughout the world
www.panmacmillan.com

ISBN 978-1-5098-2083-2

1 3 5 7 9 8 6 4 2

A CIP catalogue record for this book is available from
the British Library.

Printed and bound by CPI Group (UK) Ltd, Croydon CR0 4YY

MONDAY
14 DECEMBER 2015

There were already two people sitting outside the theater when Elena got there, so she wouldn't be first in line. But that was OK. She was still here—she was still *doing this*.

She grabbed her sleeping bag, and the backpack she'd stocked with books and food and antibacterial wipes, and got out of the car as quickly as possible; it looked like her mom might make one last attempt to talk Elena out of this.

She rolled down her window to frown at Elena directly. "I don't see a Portaloo."

Elena had said there would be a Portaloo. "I'll figure it out," Elena said quietly. "These guys are figuring it out."

"They're men," her mom said. "They can pee anywhere."

"I'll hold it," Elena said.

"For four days?"

"Mom," Elena said. And what she meant was: *We've been through this. We've talked about it for weeks and weeks. I know you don't approve. But I'm still doing it.*

Elena dropped her gear on the sidewalk, behind a tall white boy who was second in line. "OK," she said cheerfully to her mom. "I've got this. See you Thursday!"

Her mom was still frowning. "See you after lunch," she said, then rolled up her window and drove away.

Elena turned back to the line, smiling her best first-day-of-school smile. The guy next to her— he looked like he was probably about her age, seventeen or eighteen—didn't look up. First in line was a big white guy with a blond beard. He looked old enough to be one of Elena's teachers, and he was sitting in a fold-out camping chair with his feet propped up on a giant cooler. "Hey!" he said happily. "Welcome to Star Wars, man! Welcome to the line!"

This, she quickly learned, was Troy. He'd been in line since Thursday morning. "I wanted to invest at least a week in this, you know? I really wanted to gather my focus."

The younger guy, Gabe, had got in line Thursday night.

"There was a couple who hung out with us Saturday for a few hours," Troy said, "but one of them forgot her sunglasses, so they went home. Weak!"

Elena hadn't brought any sunglasses. She squinted into the sun.

"I'm guessing this is your first line," Troy said.

"How can you tell?" she asked.

"I can tell," he said, chuckling. "I can always tell. It's Gabe's first line, too."

"We were eight when the last Star Wars movie came out," Gabe said, not looking up from his book.

"*Revenge of the Sith*!" Troy said. "That wasn't much of a line anyway. It was no *Empire*."

"Nothing is," Elena said.

Troy's face got somber. "Hear, hear, Elena. Hear, hear."

All right, so . . . she'd expected there to be more people here.

The Facebook group she'd found—Camp Star Wars: Omaha!!!—had eighty-five members, not including Elena, who was more of a lurker than a joiner. This was definitely the right theater; the Facebook posts had been very clear. (Maybe it was Troy who posted them.)

Elena had planned to continue her more-lurker-than-joiner strategy in the line. She thought she'd show up and then sort of disappear into the crowd until she got her sea legs. Her line legs. It was a pretty good strategy for most social situations: show up, fall back, let somebody else break the ice and take the spotlight. Somebody else always would. Extroverts were nothing if not dependable.

But even an expert mid-trovert like Elena couldn't lie low in a crowd of three. (Though this Gabe kid seemed to be trying.) Elena was going to be here for four days. She was going to have to *talk* to these people, at least until someone else showed up.

"Cold enough for you?" Troy asked.

"Actually I think I might be little overdressed," Elena said.

She was wearing three layers on the bottom and four on top, and she had a big puffy coat if she needed it. If the temperature dropped dangerously low—which would be inevitable during a normal Omaha December—she'd have to go home. But the forecast was pretty mild. (Thanks, global warming?)

"What were they thinking when they scheduled this movie for December?" Troy said. "They weren't thinking of us, I can tell you. *May*," he said, shaking his head. "May is when you release a Star Wars movie. If this movie were a May movie, the line would already be around the block."

"Lucky for us, I guess," Elena said. "We get to be first."

"Oh, I'd be first no matter what," Troy said. "I am here for it, you know?" He cupped his hands around his lips and shouted, "I'm here for it!"

Me, too, Elena thought.

Elena couldn't remember the first time she saw a Star Wars movie . . . in the same way she couldn't remember the first time she saw her parents. Star Wars had just always *been* there. There was a stuffed Chewbacca in her crib.

The original trilogy were her dad's favorite movies—he practically knew them by heart—so when Elena was little, like four or five, she'd say they were her favorite movies, too. Because she wanted to be just like him.

And then, as she got older, the movies started to actually sink in. Like, they went from something Elena could recite to something she could *feel*. She made them her own. And then she'd kept making them her own. However Elena changed or grew, Star Wars seemed to be there for her in a new way.

When she'd found out that there were going to be sequels—*real* sequels, Han and Leia and Luke sequels—she'd flipped out. That's when she'd decided to get in line.

She didn't want to miss this moment. Not just this moment in the world, but this moment *in her life*.

If you broke Elena's heart, Star Wars would spill out. This was a holy day for her—it was a cosmic event. This was her planets lining up. (*Tatooine, Coruscant, Hoth.*)

And Elena was going to be here for it.

Her left foot was asleep.

She kept kicking the sidewalk, then stood up to bounce.

"Is your leg asleep again?" Troy said. "I'm worried about your circulation."

"It's fine," Elena said, stamping her foot.

She'd only been sitting for two hours, but she was so bored she could hardly stand it. She could literally hardly stand; even her blood vessels were bored.

She'd brought lots of books. (She'd planned to read Star Wars books whenever she had a quiet moment in line.) (Which was every moment so far.) But the wind kept blowing the pages, and the paper was so bright in the sun that reading made her eyes water.

None of that seemed to bother silent Gabe, who

read his paperback without seeming to notice the sun, the traffic, Troy, Elena or Elena's mom, who kept driving by slowly, like someone trying to buy drugs.

"The Imperial March" started playing, and Elena answered her phone.

"Why don't I pick you up now?" her mom said. "Then you can get back in line when there are more girls here."

"I'm fine," Elena said.

"You don't even know these men. They could be sexual predators."

"This doesn't seem like a very good place to prey," Elena whispered, glancing over at Gabe, who was still absorbed in his book. He was pale with curly, milk-chocolate-colored hair and rosy cheeks. He looked like Clark Kent's skinny cousin.

"You know you have to be extra careful," her mom said. "You look so young."

"We've been through this," Elena said.

They'd been through it a lot:

"*You look twelve*," her mom would say.

And Elena couldn't really argue. She was short and small. She could shop in the kids section. And the fact that she was Vietnamese seemed to scramble non-Asians' perceptions of her. She was always being mistaken for a kid.

But what was she supposed to do about that? Act like a kid until she looked like an adult? Start smoking and spend too much time in the sun?

"*Just because I look twelve doesn't mean you can treat me like I'm twelve,*" Elena would say. "*I'm going to college next year.*"

"You told me there'd be other girls here," her mom said.

"There will be."

"Good. I'll bring you back after they get here."

"I've gotta go," Elena said. "I'm trying to conserve my phone battery."

"Elena—"

"I've got to go!" Elena hung up.

The first theater employees started showing up around two. One, who looked like the manager—a Latino guy in his thirties, wearing maroon pants and a matching tie—stopped in front of the line and crossed his arms.

"So we've got a new addition, huh?"

Elena smiled.

He didn't smile back. "You know you can buy your ticket online, right?"

"I already bought my ticket," Elena said.

"Then you're guaranteed a seat. You don't have to wait in line."

"Um," Elena said. "That's OK."

"You can't talk her out of this," Troy said. "She's a true believer."

"I'm not trying to talk anybody out of anything," the manager said, looking harried. "I'm just explaining that this is an unnecessary gesture."

"All the best ones are," Troy said. "Now open the doors. My bladder is about explode."

The manager sighed. "I don't have to let you use the restroom, you know."

"Give it up, Mark," Troy said. "They tried that during *Phantom Menace*, and it didn't work then either."

"I should make you hoof it to Starbucks," the manager said, walking towards the front doors and unlocking them.

Troy stood up and made a big show of stretching. "We take turns," he said to Elena, "in line order."

She nodded.

The manager, Mark, held the door for Troy, but he was still looking at Elena. "Do your parents know you're here?"

"I'm eighteen," she said.

He looked surprised. "Well, all right. Then I

guess you're old enough to waste your own time."

Elena was hoping Gabe would open up a little while Troy was gone. They'd been sitting next to each other for hours now, and he'd only said a few words. She thought maybe he was being so quiet because he didn't want to get Troy going on one of his stories. (Troy had *so* many stories—he'd camped out for every Star Wars opening since *The Empire Strikes Back*—and he was clearly pleased to have a captive audience.)

But Gabe, with his navy-blue peacoat and his gunmetal glasses, just sat there reading about the history of polio and ignoring her.

When Troy came out with an extra-large sack of popcorn, Gabe nodded at Elena. "Go ahead."

"I'm fine," Elena said. "I just got here." She wasn't fine; she had to pee so bad she was worried she was going to leak when she stood up.

Gabe didn't move. So Elena got up and walked into the theater. The manager kept an eye on her the whole time, like she might sneak in to see a movie. She should. It was so *warm* inside the theater.

When she got back outside, Gabe took his turn.

"We have to save his spot," Troy said, "and look out for his things as if they were our own. Code of the Line." He held his bag of popcorn out over Gabe's sleeping bag.

Elena took some. "What invalidates the code?" she asked.

"What do you mean?"

"Like, are there any circumstances where someone loses their spot?"

"That is a fine question," he said. "I mean, some things are obvious. If someone takes off, without telling anyone or leaving any collateral—they're out. I think there's a time limit, too. Like, you can't just go home and take a nap and expect to come back to your spot. Everybody else is here, earning it, you know? You don't get a free pass for that. Though there are always exceptions . . ."

"There are?"

"We're human. We had a guy in the *Phantom Menace* line who had to leave for therapy. We saved his place. But another guy tried to go to work, he said he was going to lose his job . . . We pushed his tent out of line."

"You did?" Popcorn fell out of Elena's mouth. She picked it up. "That's *brutal*."

"No—" Troy was grave—"that's life. We were all going to lose our jobs. I camped out for three weeks. You think I got three weeks' vacation? At the zoo?"

"You worked at the zoo?"

"You've got to sacrifice something for this experience," Troy said, refusing to be sidetracked. "That's why we're here. You've got to leave some blood on the altar. I mean, you heard Mark. If you just want to see the new Star Wars movie, you can buy your ticket online and then forget about it until show time. But if you want to wait in line, you *wait in line*, you know?"

Elena was nodding. Gabe was standing on the sidewalk. "Did you just vote me out of the line?" he asked.

Troy laughed. "No, dude, you're good—you want some popcorn?"

Gabe took some and sat down.

Elena had been imagining this day for months. She'd been planning it for weeks.

This wasn't what she was expecting from the line experience.

This was more like being in an elevator with two random people. Like being *stuck* in an elevator.

Elena had been expecting . . . Well, more people, obviously. And more of a party. A celebration!

She'd thought it would be like all those photos she'd seen when she was a kid and the last Star Wars movies came out. All those fans out on the street, in communion with each other.

Elena had been too young to camp out then. Her dad wouldn't even let her *see* the prequels. He said she was too young. And then, when she grew up, he said they were too terrible. *"They'll just corrupt your love of Star Wars,"* he said. *"I wish I could unsee them."*

So even though Star Wars was Elena's whole life at ten, she didn't get to go to the party.

She was eighteen now. She could do whatever she wanted. *So where was the party?*

The afternoon was even more mind-numbing than the morning.

Her mom drove by three or four more times. Elena pretended not to notice. She read a few chapters of a Star Wars book. Troy pointed out that all the expanded-universe books weren't canon any more—"Disney erased them from the timeline." Elena said she didn't care, that she liked them anyway.

At nightfall, people started showing up for the evening movies, and Troy got into a fight with Mark about refilling his popcorn. "It says, '*Endless refills same day only*,'" Troy said.

"You're perverting the intent," Mark said.

Elena kept hoping that some of the people walking towards the theater were there to join the line—there were two thirty-something guys in Star Wars shirts who looked like good candidates, and a few college girls who looked nerdy enough— but they all walked right by.

Elena had stripped down to her Princess Leia T-shirt, but now that the sun was gone, she started reapplying her layers.

Maybe her mom was right. Maybe Elena should leave and come back when the line really got going . . .

What would Troy say? *There was an Asian girl who hung out with us for a few hours; then her mom made her leave.*

No, this was it. If Elena bailed, she couldn't come back.

She wrapped herself in her sleeping bag and pulled on a woolen hat with a big red pompom, taking a few more years off her appearance.

The fight with Mark seemed to leave Troy in a funk. He put in earplugs and watched Netflix on his phone. Elena watched him hungrily—she was dying to use her phone. Her whole world was in there. Sitting outside in the cold and dark would be so much more bearable if she could read fanfiction or text her friends. But she only had one back-up battery pack to last four days . . . At least it was still bright enough to read. She was sitting just below a lit up Star Wars poster.

Her mom pulled up in front of the theater again at ten. Elena got up and walked to the car.

"I don't like this," her mom said. "People are going to think you're homeless."

"No one will think that."

"Homeless people are going to bother you."

"Probably not."

"I talked to Dì Janet and she says you can buy your movie ticket online."

"That's not the point."

"It's just that—" Her mom rubbed her temple. "Elena, I think this is the dumbest thing you've ever done in your life."

"That's a good thing, Mom. Think about how much worse it could be."

Her mom frowned and handed her a warm covered dish. "You answer your texts tonight."

"I will."

Elena stepped away from the car.

"Don't worry about her!" Troy shouted from behind her. "She's in good hands!"

Elena's mom looked aghast. But she still drove away.

"I'm sorry," Troy said. "Did I make that worse? I meant the hands of the line."

"It's OK," Elena said, finding her spot against the wall.

Mark the theater manager came out one more time to give them a last call for the bathroom and concessions, which was pretty decent of him.

Troy was asleep by eleven, stretched out on his chair with an inflatable pillow wedged between him and the wall. He'd wrapped himself in fleece blankets, tipped his head back, and that was it.

Elena had planned to roll out her sleeping bag and sleep lying down. But that was back when she'd imagined a few dozen campers. It was different with just three people, and she felt too exposed at the end of the line. If she fell asleep lying down, someone could just drag her away in the night, and Troy and Gabe would never notice.

She didn't think she was afraid of Troy and Gabe themselves. Troy hadn't said anything pervy yet. Not even about Princess Leia. And Gabe seemed painstakingly uninterested in Elena.

Her mom didn't trust them, but her mom didn't trust any guys. She used to just have it in for white guys. ("*White guys are the worst. They rap 2 Live Crew lyrics at you and expect you to laugh.*") But ever since she and Elena's dad had separated four years ago, her mom had taken a stand against any and every man, especially where Elena was concerned. *"Learn from my mistakes,"* she said.

Learn what? Elena wondered. Avoid men? Avoid love? Avoid radiologists who buy movie-replica lightsabers?

Usually when her mom gave her warnings like this, Elena would just give her a thumbs up. Like, *No prob, Bob.*

Because it really wasn't a problem. Avoid men? Done! This had literally never been an issue for her. When other girls complained about how to deal with unwanted male attention, Elena wouldn't feel jealous exactly, but she would feel curious—how does one go about attracting such attention? And is it impossible to attract just some of it? Just a small, manageable amount? Or was attention from boys all or nothing, like a tap that, once you'd found it, you could never turn off?

Elena's teeth were starting to chatter, and it wasn't even that cold out. But the cold of the ground had crept through her sleeping bag, through her jeans, through her long underwear and tights, and settled into her bones.

"You've gotta put something under your

sleeping bag," Gabe said. "Or get off the ground."

She looked where his butt must be. He lifted the side of his sleeping bag up. He was sitting on cardboard, two or three pieces.

"Does that work?" she asked.

"It helps," he said.

"Well, I don't have a spare box on me . . ."

Gabe sighed. "Hold my spot."

He got up and shuffled out of his sleeping bag, walking down the street and disappearing behind the building. When he came back, he was carrying a few cardboard boxes. Raisinets. Sour Patch Kids.

"You take mine," he said.

"What?"

"Move up, unless you don't want to sit between us. Troy's an excellent windbreak."

Elena shuffled over to Gabe's pile of boxes, pulling her things with her. Gabe quickly made himself a new nest and settled down again.

"It does help," Elena said. "Thanks."

She tested her instincts, to see if she felt any less safe sitting between these two strangers than on the end. No. She felt about the same. "You just want *me* to have to listen to Troy's stories," she whispered.

"We can switch back in the morning," he said.

"Do you know him?" she asked. "Troy?"

"I didn't know him before," Gabe said, "but I have been sitting next to him for four days . . ."

Gabe picked up his book.

"Thanks," Elena said again.

Gabe didn't answer.

TUESDAY
15 DECEMBER 2015

It didn't seem like Elena had slept, but she must have. She woke up slumped over her backpack with a patch of cold saliva on her chin.

"Star Wars!" someone was shouting from a car driving by.

"Star Wars!" Troy shouted back, raising his fist.

Yes, Elena thought, *Star Wars*. That's what this experience needed: more Star Wars.

Elena was going to rally.

So this wasn't the jubilant, communal, public display of affection she'd been expecting—it could still be *something*. It could still be memorable. She'd make it memorable.

"What does the Code of the Line say about going to Starbucks?" she asked.

Troy answered: "Totally acceptable as long as you bring back some for us."

Elena walked the six blocks to Starbucks and hung out in the bathroom for a while, painting little Yodas on her cheeks. She had the Starbucks barista write character names on their cups. Troy was Admiral Ackbar, Gabe was General Dodonna, and Elena was Mon Mothma.

When she got back to the line, she took out her phone and carefully took a selfie of herself with the guys behind her. Gabe wouldn't look at the camera, but Troy played along. *"Third in line!"* Elena posted on Instagram. Which sounded much better than *"Last in Line!"*

"I dig your face paint," Troy said. "I've got a costume, but I'm saving it for opening night."

"Do you always wear a costume on opening night?" Elena asked.

"Oh yeah. Usually I camp in it."

"I want to hear about your costumes," Elena said.

"You mean opening-night costumes? Or all my Star Wars costumes, including Halloween and May the Fourth parties?"

"We want to hear about *all* of them," she said, glancing over at Gabe. "Right?"

Gabe was looking at her like she was out of her mind.

After they got through Troy's costumes, Elena quizzed him about highs and lows from past lines. Then she suggested they play Star Wars trivia, which she quickly realized wasn't a good idea, because she couldn't answer any questions about the prequels, and she didn't want Troy and Gabe to guess that she hadn't actually seen them.

Elena *could* have seen them by now. She could have watched all three prequels after her dad moved to Florida—but it still felt like she'd be betraying him. And even though her dad had betrayed her by leaving, she didn't feel like watching Star Wars movies just to spite him. That seemed like it really *would* corrupt her love for Star Wars. "*A Jedi uses the Force for knowledge and defense, never for attack.*" (Yoda.)

Elena's mom drove by a few times that morning. Elena just waved and tried to look like she was having the time of her life.

Nobody new got in line.

The highlight of Tuesday afternoon was when a photographer from the newspaper came by to take their picture.

"I'm looking for the Star Wars line," he said. He had an oversized camera with a long black lens.

"That's us!" Troy said.

"Oh." He squinted at them. "I thought there was supposed to be a real line, like with people in costume."

"Come back on opening night," Troy said. "My Poe Dameron will knock your socks off."

The photographer looked at Elena's cheeks. "Is that Shrek?"

"It's Yoda," Gabe snapped. "For Christ's sake."

In the end, the photographer shot a close-up of Troy holding a photo of himself waiting in a much more interesting line fifteen years ago.

It was a humiliating setback for them as individuals and for the line as a whole.

(Ugh. They weren't a *line*. They were just three cold nerds.) (They were three suckers who showed up for a party that didn't exist.) (They were statistically insignificant!)

After the photographer left, Elena didn't start another cheerful conversation. Gabe excused himself to walk around the block. Troy watched TV on his phone.

Elena took out her phone just long enough to take a photo of her flowered sneakers. "*My legs are permanently asleep*," she posted. "*#LineProblems*." Then she immediately put her phone away, before she could start wandering around online and enjoying herself.

When Gabe came back he was frowning more than Elena had ever seen a human being frown. Even her mother. It was the longest afternoon of her life.

By Tuesday evening, deep malaise had set in. Luke-staring-into-both-suns-of-Tatooine malaise.

Elena hid her face whenever movie-goers walked by. She only perked up when her mom came by around ten. *Gotta keep up appearances.*

When Elena stood up to go to the car, her whole body felt numb with cold and disuse. Her mom shoved a hot-water bottle out the window. "Here."

It was so hot that Elena dropped it. "Thanks," she said, picking it up.

"I don't think George Lucas would want you to do this," her mom said.

"I didn't know you knew who George Lucas was."

"Please. I was watching Star Wars movies before you were born. Your dad and I saw *Empire Strikes Back* five times in the theater."

"Lucky," Elena said.

"George Lucas is a father of daughters," her mother said. "He wouldn't want young girls freezing to death to prove their loyalty."

"This isn't about George Lucas," Elena said. "He isn't even that involved in the sequels."

"Come home," her mom said. "We'll watch *Empire Strikes Back* and I'll make hot cocoa."

"I can't," Elena said. "I'll lose my place in line."

"I think it will still be there for you in the morning."

"Goodnight, Mom."

Her mom sighed and held out a venti Starbucks cup "Stay warm. I'll leave my ringer on tonight in case you change your mind."

Elena sat down with her coffee and tucked the hot-water bottle into her sleeping bag. It felt *amazing*.

"Call your Mom," Gabe said flatly. "I want to watch *Empire Strikes Back* and drink hot cocoa."

She realized now that the coffee was a set-up.

It was two in the morning, and Elena was going to wet her pants. She looked up the line. Troy was wrapped in sleeping bags and a polar fleece, like a mummy. Gabe had pulled his knees up and tucked his head down a few hours ago.

Elena had been sleeping. Badly. She felt groggy and out of sorts and her bladder actually *hurt*. She kept fidgeting. Gabe lifted his head. "What's wrong? Are you cold?"

"No," Elena said. "I mean, yes, of course. But no—I'm going to wet my pants."

"Don't do that," Gabe said.

"*I can't help it*. What am I supposed to do?"

"Go pee somewhere."

"Where?"

"I don't know. Behind a car or something."

"That's illegal!" Elena said. "And gross!"

"Not as gross as peeing your pants."

Elena closed her eyes. "Ughhhhhhhhhhh. Where have you guys been peeing?"

"Inside the theater," he said.

"Don't you ever have to go at night?"

He shrugged. "No."

Elena felt tears rolling down her cheeks.

"Don't cry," Gabe said. "That won't help."

She kept crying. It was going to happen soon.

"OK," he said, standing up. "Come on."

"Where are we going?"

"To let you pee."

"We can't leave without telling Troy," she said. "Code of the Line."

"The Code of the Line also includes not soiling it. Come on."

Troy had an extra-large Coke cup, and Gabe grabbed it. Elena got up, carefully, and followed him around to the back of the theater.

"OK," he said, holding out the cup. "You go behind the dumpster, pee in this cup, then put it in the dumpster."

"What if there are cameras?" Elena said, taking the cup.

"I can't help you there. This isn't *Mission: Impossible*, you know?"

"But what if I need to pee more than this?

I don't know how much I pee."

"If your bladder held more than forty-four ounces, you wouldn't have to go to the bathroom constantly."

She stood there, biting her lip.

"Elena."

"Yeah?"

"You don't have any other options here. Pee in the cup."

"Right," she said. She walked, carefully, to the other side of the dumpster. "I don't want you to listen!"

"Is this the first time you've peed around another human being?"

"Around a guy," she shouted, "yes!"

"I didn't ask for this!" Gabe shouted back. He started humming loudly—"The Imperial March". It made Elena feel like her mom was coming.

She carefully peeled down her layers and hovered over the cup, trying not to touch it, and trying not to splash, still sort of crying. Gabe kept up the loud humming. When Elena was done, she put the lid on the cup and walked out. "OK," she said.

"Gross. You were supposed to throw it away."

"I'm going to pour it down a storm drain! So it doesn't spill on anyone."

"Whatever," Gabe said.

When she'd disposed of the pee, and the cup, she sat back down next to him and dug in her bag for a wet wipe.

"I should just go home," she said, scrubbing her hands.

"Do you have to pee again?"

"No."

"Then why do you want to go home?"

"Well, obviously I'm not prepared for this!" She waved her arm around, encompassing the cold, the line, the trash can, the storm drain . . . "And it isn't how I thought it was going to be."

"How'd you think it was going to be?" Gabe asked.

"I don't know—*fun*."

"You're camping on a sidewalk with strangers. Why would that be fun?"

"It always *looks* fun. In the pictures. Like, tent cities. And people meeting in line and making friends for life. Getting matching tattoos."

"You want to get a matching tattoo with Troy?"

"You know what I mean." She threw her wadded-up wet wipe on to the ground. "I thought it was going to be a celebration, like a way to be really excited about Star Wars with a bunch of other people who are really excited about Star

Wars. Like in Troy's stories. Like the time they all camped out for two weeks to see *Return of the Jedi* and ended up with soulmates and nicknames. The practical jokes that went on for days! The lightsaber battles!"

"You could still end up with a nickname," Gabe said. "Right now I'm thinking something to do with pee. Or cups."

Elena wrapped her sleeping bag tighter.

"Good Old Pees-in-a-Cup," Gabe said.

"Why are you here?" she asked. "If you knew it was going to be miserable."

"I'm here because I love Star Wars," he said. "Same as you." He folded his arms on his knees and tucked his head down.

"But you don't even talk to me," Elena said. "To either of us."

Gabe made a sarcastic noise, like *hrmph*.

"No, seriously," she said. "What's the point of getting in this line if you don't want to experience it with other people?"

"Maybe I just don't want to experience it with you," he said. "Have you thought of that?"

"Oh my God." She scrunched up her face. "*No.* I haven't thought of that. Is that true? Why are you so mean?"

"It's not true," he grumbled, lifting his head.

"I'm just tired. And I'm not—a people person. Sorry I'm not meeting your Star Wars dream line expectations."

"Me, too." She rubbed her hands together and blew in them.

"Why didn't your friends wait in line with you?" Gabe said. "Then you could have had your party line."

"None of my friends likes Star Wars."

"Everybody likes Star Wars," he said. "Everybody likes everything these days. The whole world is a nerd."

"Are you mad because other people like Star Wars? Are you mad because people *like me* like Star Wars?"

Gabe glowered at her. "Maybe."

"Well," she said, "my friends *do* like Star Wars. They're going to see it this weekend. But they don't like it like I do. They don't get a stomach ache about it."

"Why does Star Wars give you a stomach ache?"

"I don't know. I just care about it so much."

"I wasn't trying to call you a fake geek girl," Gabe said.

"I didn't say that you were."

"I mean, you obviously know the original

trilogy inside out. And that's not even important, but you obviously do."

"I've yet to determine whether you're a fake geek boy," she said, pulling her sleeves down over her hands.

He laughed, and she was ninety per cent sure it wasn't sarcastic.

"Here's what bothers me," he said, glowering slightly less, but still looking frustrated. "I'm a nerd, right? Like obviously. Classic nerd. I hate sports. I know every Weird Al song by heart. I don't know how to talk to most people. I'm probably going to get a job in computer science. Like, I know those are all stereotypes, but they're also true of me. That's who I am. And the thing about nerd culture being mainstream culture now means that there's no place to just be a nerd among other nerds—without being reminded that you're the nerd. Do you follow me?"

"Only sort of," Elena said.

"OK. So. If I go to a football party at my brother's house, I don't know anything about football, and I'm the nerd. And if I go dancing with my friend who likes to dance, well, I don't dance, and I don't like loud music, so I'm the nerd. But *now*, even if I go see a comic-book movie, the whole world is there—so I'm still the nerd. I would have thought that a *Star Wars line* would be safe," he said, waving his arm around the way Elena had. "No way am I going to feel like a social outcast in a Star Wars line. No way am I going to have to sit next to one of the *cool girls* for four days."

"Whoa," Elena said. "I'm not a cool girl."

"Give me a break."

She held up her index finger. "I feel like I need to say that everyone should be welcome in a Star Wars line, socially successful or not, but also, *whoa*. I am a nerd," she said. "That's what this was supposed to be, a chance to talk to people who wouldn't care that I'm awkward in literally every other situation."

"That's not true," he said, rolling his eyes.

"It is."

"You have friends. You have a clique. You walk down the hall like you own the place."

"You seem to have mistaken me for the movie *Mean Girls*," Elena said. "Also, are you saying you don't have friends at your school? Have you considered that maybe it's your silent pouting that drives people away?"

"I have friends," Gabe said. "That's not the point."

"So you have *friends*, but you think I have a *clique*."

"I'm pretty sure of it."

"I feel like you're projecting your clearly problematic girl issues on me," she said.

Gabe rolled his eyes again. "I thought you said you couldn't talk to people," he said. "You don't seem to have any problems talking to me."

"I'm having *a lot* of problems talking to you."

"OK, then, let's stop."

Was Gabe really mad? She couldn't tell.

Was Elena mad? She also couldn't tell . . .

Yes. *Yes*, Elena *was* mad. Who was Gabe to take her inventory like this? He didn't know her. And he was giving her zero benefit of the doubt; she'd been giving him nothing *but* benefit of the doubt for thirty-six hours.

"For what it's worth," she said, without looking at him, "I haven't thought, *Whoa, Gabe sure is a nerd*, even once since I sat down."

He didn't say anything.

Elena squirmed. She wrapped her sleeping bag as tightly as she could and rearranged her legs. "Ugggggggggch."

"I get it," he said. "You think I'm a jerk."

"No. *Yes*, but no—I have to pee again."

"You just went."

"I know, I can't help it. Sometimes it happens in waves."

"Can you wait?"

"*No.*"

Gabe sighed and stood up. "Come on. Let's go back to the dumpster."

"I threw away the cup!" Elena said.

"You still have your hot-water bottle—"

"*No.*"

Gabe clicked his tongue like he was thinking. Elena started rooting through her backpack. Everything she'd brought was in plastic bags.

"Aha!" Gabe said. He reached behind her sleeping bag and pulled out her Starbucks cup. "This is perfect," he said. "It's already got your name on it."

They left their sleeping bags and shuffled to the back of the theater again. It was no less humiliating the second time around.

"You're definitely getting a nickname," Gabe said when she sat down again.

Elena crawled into her sleeping bag, feeling more unbelievably tired than unbelievably uncomfortable, like maybe she'd be able to get some sleep for real now.

"I was born at the wrong time," she said. "And in the wrong climate. It should be 1983, and I should be sitting outside Mann's Chinese Theatre in Hollywood, California."

"They're camping outside the Chinese Theatre tonight," Gabe said. "Troy says we're all one line."

"I'm probably last in that one, too," Elena said. She rolled away from Gabe and fell asleep.

WEDNESDAY
16 DECEMBER 2015

"The Force awakens!" Troy shouted.

Elena pulled her hat down over her eyes.

"Come on, Elena," Troy said. "We're hoping you'll get coffee again."

"Because I'm a woman?"

"No. Because you probably have to pee," Gabe said.

Elena did. "Fine, tell me what you want."

Twenty minutes later she was staring at herself in the Starbucks mirror. She was starting to look like someone who slept on the street and washed up in Starbucks bathrooms.

There'd been an actual homeless person sitting outside the Starbucks when Elena walked in, and it made her feel like a big creep to think she was doing this for fun. (It wasn't even fun!)

She told the barista their names were "Tarkin", "Veers" and "Ozzel".

"Feeling your dark side today, huh?" Troy said when she handed him his cup.

"Pretty much," Elena said, dropping to the ground. "Fear, anger, hate, suffering . . ."

"T-minus one!" Troy said. "One more day. *One more day!* I can't believe we've waited ten years for this, though honestly I never thought it would come. *Real* sequels . . ."

"What's your favorite Star Wars movie?" Gabe asked. Uncharacteristically. Elena looked over at him.

"You might as well ask me who my favorite child is," Troy said.

"Do you have children?" Elena asked him.

"I meant hypothetically," Troy said. He exhaled hard. "This is tough, this is really tough. I'm going to have to go with *The Empire Strikes Back*."

The next half-hour was taken up by Troy justifying his choice. At several points he considered changing his answer, but he kept landing back on Hoth.

"What about you, Elena?" Gabe finally asked.

She frowned at him. Suspicious. "*Empire*," she said. "For all the reasons Troy just said. Plus the kissing. What's yours?"

"*Episode Six*," Gabe said.

"*Jedi*?" she asked.

He nodded.

"Solid choice," Troy said. "Very solid."

Gabe didn't expound; instead he turned back to

Elena. "So, what's your least favorite?"

"Why do I have to go first?"

"You don't have to," he said.

She held her coffee cup in both hands. "No, it's fine. *Jedi*. I still love it. But yeah."

Troy acted like he'd been shot. "*Jedi*?"

Gabe was shocked, too. "You think *Episode Six* is worse than *Episode Two*? Worse than Anakin and Padmé frolicking among the shaaks?"

"The shaaks!" Troy said. "Geonosis!"

Those sounded like nonsense words to Elena. She didn't want to be found out. She bit her lip. "I wasn't really considering the prequels. You said least *favorite*, not worst."

"Ahhhh," Troy said, "you did say that."

"True," Gabe said.

They moved on to Troy's least favorite (*III*— "the violence just struck me as mindless") and then to Gabe's (*II*—"love on the fields of Naboo").

And then Troy had to take a call from his girlfriend.

"So," Gabe said to Elena, "who's your favorite character?"

"What are you doing?" Elena said.

"Talking about Star Wars."

"Why?"

"I thought this was what you wanted."

"So now you're trying to give me what I want?"

Gabe sighed. "Not exactly. Just . . . maybe you were right."

"When?" she asked.

"When you said that the point of being in this line was to be excited about Star Wars with other people who love Star Wars."

"Of course I was right," Elena said. "That's obviously why people camp out like this. Nobody leaves their house to sit outside a theater for a week just so they can ignore other fans."

"So I was getting in my own way," Gabe admitted. "OK?"

"OK," Elena said carefully.

"So, who's your favorite character?" he asked again.

"You'll probably think it's basic."

"I'm not a jerk," he said.

"People who are jerks don't get to decide whether they're jerks. It's left up to a jury of their peers."

"I disagree. I do not identify as a jerk, so I'm not going to act like one."

"Fine," Elena said. "Princess Leia."

"Great choice," he said.

She was still suspicious. "What about you?"

*

The thing about Gabe being nice to Elena for unknown, suspicious reasons was . . . he was still being nice to her. And interesting. And funny. And good company.

She kept forgetting that it was all an act and possibly a ruse—and just enjoyed herself.

They were *all* enjoying themselves.

"Excuse me," someone said, interrupting a lively discussion about whom they'd each buy a drink for in the cantina.

The whole line looked up. There were two women standing on the sidewalk with bakery boxes. One of them cleared her throat. "We heard that people were camping out for Star Wars . . ."

"That's us!" Troy said, only slightly less enthusiastically than he'd said it yesterday.

"Where's everybody else?" she asked. "Are they around the back? Do you do this in shifts?"

"It's just us," Elena said.

"We're the Cupcake Gals," the other woman said. "We thought we'd bring Star Wars cupcakes? For the line?"

"Great!" Troy said.

The Cupcake Gals held on tight to their boxes.

"It's just . . ." the first woman said, "we were going to take a photo of the whole line, and post it on Instagram . . ."

"I can help you there!" Elena said. Those cupcakes were not going to just walk away. Not on Elena's watch.

Elena took a selfie of their line, the Cupcake Gals and a theater employee all holding Star Wars cupcakes—it looked like a snapshot from a crowd—and promised to post it across all her channels. The lighting was perfect. Magic hour, no filter necessary. *#CupcakeGals #TheForceACAKEns #SalaciousCrumbs*

The Gals were completely satisfied and left both boxes of cupcakes.

"This is the first time I've been happy that there were only three of us," Elena said, helping herself to a second cupcake. It was frosted to look like Chewbacca.

"You *saved* these cupcakes," Gabe said. "Those women were going to walk away with them."

"I know," Elena said. "I could see it in their eyes. I would've stopped at nothing to change their minds."

"Thank God they were satisfied by a selfie then," Gabe said. His cupcake looked like Darth Vader, and his tongue was black.

"I'm really good at selfies," Elena said. "Especially for someone with short arms."

"Great job," Troy said. "You'll make someone

a great provider someday."

"That day is today," Elena said, leaning back against the theater wall. "You're both welcome."

"Errrggh," Troy said, kicking his feet out. "Cupcake coma."

"How many did you eat?" Gabe asked.

"Four," Troy said. "I took down the Jedi Council. Time for a little midday siesta—the Force *asleepens*."

It was the warmest day yet. Elena wondered if she could take a nap too. Maybe not. It seemed even weirder to be asleep on the street in the middle of the day than at night.

"You hate the prequels more than anyone I've met," Gabe said, licking his thumb. "These cupcakes are really good. You should tweet about them again."

"I don't hate the prequels," she said.

"We ranked our top thirty characters, and the only prequel character you listed was Queen Amidala."

That was the only prequel character Elena *knew* . . .

"I mean you must really *hate* them," he said.

"All right," she said, "I feel like I owe you a debt, after you helped me last night—"

"You do," Gabe said. "Not quite a life debt. But

I did save you from peeing your pants *twice*."

"So I'm going to tell you a secret," she said. "But you have to promise not to use it against me."

Gabe reached over Elena's legs to get another cupcake. "How could you possibly have a dark secret involving the Star Wars sequels? Are you responsible for Jar Jar Binks?"

"Do you promise?" she asked.

"Sure, I promise."

"I've never seen the prequels."

"*What?*" Gabe spit crumbs all over both of them. Elena shook them out of her ponytail. "How could that happen?"

"It didn't happen," she said. "I never saw them."

"Was it against your religion? Are you some sort of Star Wars purist?"

"Sort of," Elena said. "My dad was. He wouldn't let me see them."

"Did he lock you in a tower?"

"No. He just told me they were terrible. He said they'd . . . *corrupt* my love of Star Wars."

"And you never thought of watching them anyway?"

"Not really. It's my *dad*."

"How does he feel about the sequels? Are you here undercover?"

"I don't know," Elena said. "I haven't heard from him."

Gabe looked confused.

"He's sort of in Florida."

"'Sort of in Florida' is our band name," Gabe said.

"Don't tell Troy," she said.

"I won't. He'd probably make us watch them all on his phone."

Elena looked down. "Now you're probably thinking that I really am a fake geek girl."

"I try not to think that about anybody," he said. "If anything, this makes you an uber Star Wars nerd. A Star Wars hipster. You're like one of those people who only listens to music on vinyl."

"Do you think I should watch the prequels?" she asked.

"How would I know? I mean, I'd watch them. I couldn't know there was more Star Wars out there that I hadn't tapped. You could have double the Star Wars in your life."

"Did the prequels corrupt your love of Star Wars?"

Gabe gave her a very Han Solo-like grin. "It was already corrupt, babe."

They both laughed. This was not the Gabe she'd been sitting next to for two days.

"I don't know," he said, more seriously. "I saw the prequels before the original trilogy."

"What?" It was Elena's turn to be shocked. "That's all wrong. That's a perversion."

"It is not!" Gabe said. "I think it's how George Lucas intended it. It's the higher order."

"George Lucas doesn't even know what he intended," Elena said. "He can't even decide who shot first."

"I saw the prequels in the theater," Gabe said. "When I was a kid. I thought they were awesome."

"And now?" she asked.

"They're my first love," he said. "I can't be objective."

Elena hugged herself. "I don't think I'll ever see them. I feel like I'd be letting my dad down. Like he's going to show up some day, and ask whether I've seen *Attack of the Clones*, and if I say yes, he'll take off again."

Gabe looked like he was thinking. "So . . ." he said, "you won't mind if I spoil them for you."

"I guess not," she said. "I mean, I already know what happens."

Gabe sat up straight and held both hands up between them. "*Turmoil has engulfed the Great Republic . . .*"

*

When Troy woke up from his nap, he didn't even ask what they were doing. He just joined in. His Yoda impression was *uncanny*.

"I knew you hadn't seen the prequels," Troy confided in Elena. "There were some pretty obvious gaps in your understanding of the Galactic Senate."

Troy's girlfriend, Sandra, brought them all pizza that night, and when she got there she joined the dramatic re-enactment. She said they had to rewind so she could elaborate for Elena on how dashing Obi-Wan was. "*Ewan McGregor*," she groaned. "I made Troy grow a beard after the second movie."

"I also grew a Padawan braid," Troy said.

Troy and Sandra and Gabe acted out a lightsaber battle that brought tears to Elena's eyes, probably because they were all three singing the John Williams music. (Elena knew the prequel music; she'd listened to all the scores.)

Some movie-goers stopped on their way out of the theater to watch. Elena snapped a photo when Gabe fell to the ground. (*#Epic #KnightFall #OnLine*) Everyone clapped.

When the crowd cleared, Elena noticed her mom parked at the curb. Elena jumped up and ran over.

"Are you coming home?" her mom asked.

"Nope," Elena said. "Do you want to get in line?"

"No way. You get this craziness from your dad, not me."

The night was clear and cold. Sandra had talked Manager Mark into refilling Elena's hot-water bottle at the coffee machine. Elena hugged it under her sleeping bag.

"Hey," Gabe said, "I got you something."

"What?"

He handed her a movie-theater cup, one of the new Star Wars ones. "Tonight you can pee in a collector's item."

"Ha ha," Elena said. "Did we eat all the cupcakes?"

Gabe handed her the box. There was one left. A very lonely C-3PO. Elena picked up her phone and took a photo of it. Then went to Instagram. *#LastDroidStanding*

Her phone battery was still seventy per cent charged, and she only had twenty-four hours to get through, so Elena decided to indulge herself by thumbing through her Instagram feed, reading the comments on her posts from the last few days.

Her friends had all hearted them and left funny

comments. God, Elena missed her friends. (Not that Troy and Gabe weren't great. She'd definitely miss them.) (Even Gabe.) (Especially Gabe.)

Her first post, from Monday, had the most comments. The photo of the line.

"Is that Gabe?" someone had posted.

"GABERS."

"It's Geekle!" Elena's friend Jocelyn had posted. *"ICKLE GEEKLE."*

Geekle? Elena thought.

She quickly texted Jocelyn: *"Who's Geekle?"*

"Geekle!" Jocelyn texted back. *"From Spanish class. He sits at the back. He's kind of geeky."*

"Is that why you call him Geekle?"

"IDK," Jocelyn sent. *"ICKLE GEEKLE. Tell him I said hi."*

Elena looked at Gabe. He did look sort of familiar. Now that she thought about it. Jocelyn had nicknames for everyone, usually mean ones. Ickle Geekle, whatever that meant, was mild. Jocelyn herself wasn't very mean, once you got to know her. She just thought she was funnier than she actually was. And she couldn't stand silence. She'd fill every second with stupid jokes.

Gabe. From Spanish class. Elena pictured him without his peacoat . . . While she was staring, Gabe took off his glasses and rubbed his eyes.

"You don't wear glasses!" she blurted.

"What?" he said, putting his glasses back on.

"In school," she said. "You don't wear glasses."

Gabe's face fell. "No. I don't."

Gabe. Geekle. His Spanish name was *Gabriel*. She'd never talked to him; she'd never really looked at him. (Which sounded worse than it was—Elena didn't go around *looking* at people. She minded her own business!)

This was bad. This was very bad.

"I'm sorry," she said.

"Why?"

"I didn't recognize you."

"Why would you?" he said.

"We're in class together!"

"You apparently never noticed. There's no crime there."

"Did you recognize me?"

Gabe turned to look at her. "*Of course.*" He rolled his eyes. "We've been in school together for four years."

"I don't know very many people."

"Why should you?" he said. "You've got your clique."

That was true, but not the way he was saying it. "We're not a clique," she said.

"Gang, then."

"Gabe."

"Army?"

"Why do you dislike us so much?"

"Because you're jerks," he said. "Because you call me Geekle— what does that even mean?"

"I don't know. I don't call you that!"

"Because you don't know I exist!"

"I know *now*," she said.

Gabe started to say something, then shook his head.

"Jocelyn has a big mouth," Elena said. "She's harmless."

"To you," Gabe said. "You guys think you're so far above everyone else."

"I don't think that."

"You walk around in a clump, looking all cute and matchy, and throw your clever little insults down on us plebes—"

"We never intentionally match!" Elena said.

"Whatever!"

They both sat back, arms crossed.

"It's not like that," Elena said. "We're not a clique. We're just friends."

Gabe huffed. "Do you know why I know you and your friends? But you don't know me and my friends?"

"Why?"

"Because we don't get in your way. We don't have nicknames for you, and if we did, we wouldn't shout them every day when you walked into Spanish."

"That's just Jocelyn," Elena said.

"That's your whole vibe," Gabe said.

"I don't even have a vibe!"

"Pfft!"

"So you hate me," she said. "You hated me before I even got in line."

"I didn't hate you," he said. "You're just . . . part of them."

"I'm also part of this," she said.

"What's this? Star Wars? I don't have to like you because you like Star Wars. I don't have to like every meathead with a stormtrooper tattoo."

"No," Elena said. "I'm part of this, part of the line."

"What does that count for?"

"I don't know," she said, "but it should count for something. Look, I'm sorry Jocelyn calls you names. She's a loudmouth. She's been a loudmouth since fourth grade. We're all just *used* to her. And if you've noticed me at all at school, you've noticed that I don't exactly reach out. I don't talk to anybody in some of my classes. There's nobody in my math class who could pick me out of a line-up."

"I don't believe that," he said.

"I'm sorry," she said, "that I've never talked to you before. But you've never talked to me either. We're talking *now*."

Gabe gritted his teeth. "I *hate* it when she calls me Geekle."

"She calls me Ele-nerd," Elena said. "And Short Stuff. Wednesday Addams. Virgin Daiquiri. Ukelena . . . Ukelele. Lele. My Little Pony. Thumbelina. Rumpelstiltskin . . ."

Gabe laughed a little. "Why do you let her call you all that?"

"I don't even hear it any more," Elena said. "Plus it's different. I'm her friend . . . I can have her stop calling you names, if you want?"

"It doesn't even matter," Gabe said.

They were quiet for a minute. Elena was trying to figure out whether she was mad. She wasn't.

"Why didn't you tell me?" she asked. "That we already knew each other."

"I didn't want you to call me Geekle," Gabe said. "I didn't want it to catch on."

Elena nodded.

"We should sleep," he said. "This is our last night."

"Yeah," Elena said.

He pulled up his legs and folded his arms. *How did he sleep like that?*

Elena curled up as much as she could. She kept trying to get comfortable. It was so bright under the lights.

"Gabe?" she said after ten minutes or so.

"Yeah?"

"Are you asleep?"

"Sort of."

"Are you still mad?"

Gabe sighed. "In a larger sense, yes. At you, in this moment, no."

"OK. Good."

Elena hunkered down again. She watched the cars driving by. She would be really, really glad to be home tomorrow night. After the movie. The movie . . .

"Gabe?" she said.

"What?"

"I can't sleep."

"Why not?"

"Star Wars!"

THURSDAY
17 DECEMBER 2015

Something strange happened at 6 a.m.

Darth Vader got in line.

It was one of Troy's friends. He kicked Troy's feet off the cooler and shouted, "The Force awakens!"

"Yeah, we've heard that one," Gabe grumbled, sitting up.

Elena was watching everything from a gap between her hat and her sleeping bag.

"I haven't slept in a week," Gabe said. "I think you can die of that. I think I'm dead."

Troy woke up and welcomed his friend, who eventually got in line behind Gabe.

Elena and Gabe walked together to Starbucks. She gave him some of her baby wipes; they were both in dire need of a shower. Gabe looked like he was growing a beard. It was coming in redder than his hair. Elena painted new Yodas on her cheeks.

"You into Star Wars?" the barista asked.

"Nope," Gabe said.

"Yes," Elena said.

"I'm going to see it tonight," the barista said. "Midnight showing."

"Cool," Elena said.

"There are already people in line over there," he said. "Have you seen them? Just three miserable dorks sitting on the sidewalk."

Elena smiled brightly. "That's us!"

"What?"

"We're the three dorks—well, two of the three."

The barista was mortified; he gave them their coffee for free. "May the Force be with you!" Elena said.

When they got back, there were three new people in line.

By noon, there were twenty, at least half of them in costume.

By three, there were speakers on the sidewalk, and someone kept playing the victory parade music from *The Phantom Menace* over and over again. (It was only a minute and a half long.)

Elena consented to a ninety-second dance with Troy. Gabe turned him down.

Fifty people showed up by dinner time, and some of them brought pizza. Elena went up and down the line, posing for photos and posting them to Instagram. (Her hashtags were *inspired*.) Troy, who'd changed into his pilot costume, was a little wary of all the newcomers—"Jar-Jar-come-latelies."

"We have to keep our guard up," he said. "These people aren't part of the line covenant. They might try to surge at the end."

"We still have our tickets," Gabe said.

"I will be the first person to walk into that theater," Troy said. "You will be second. And Elena will be third. We are the line. These are just day guests."

"So are we sitting together?" Elena asked.

"Oh," Troy said. "Well, we can sit near each other. I've actually got a bunch of friends coming . . ."

"We can sit together," Gabe said, looking at Elena, but somehow *not* looking at Elena. "If you want."

"Sure," she said. "Let's see this through."

The newspaper photographer came back. The line wrapped around the block. Mark came out with a loudspeaker to give everybody directions.

"We've got two hours," Gabe said to Elena. "I think we've only got time for a tattoo *or* a nickname. Your pick."

"Let's not talk about nicknames," she said.

They'd packed up their stuff and Mark said they could leave it in his office during the movie. "Thank you for not being drunk or disorderly," he said. "And for not littering. I hope you camp outside a different theater next time—I'd be happy to make a few recommendations."

"No chance," Troy said. "This is home."

Elena bounced up and down, pointing from side to side.

"What's that?" Gabe asked.

"It's my Star Wars dance," she said, bouncing and pointing.

After a few seconds, he joined her. Then Troy's friends picked it up. The dance traveled down the line. From the street, they must have looked like the Peanuts characters dancing.

There *was* a surge at the end—Troy was right! The line turned into a mob when Mark opened the doors. But Mark shouted at everyone and made sure the three original line members got in first. Gabe and Elena grabbed seats in the very middle of the theater.

"Oh my God," Elena said. "This is the most

comfortable chair I've ever sat in. I feel like a princess."

"You look like a ruffian," Gabe said, but his eyes were closed. "It's so warm," he said. "I love inside."

"Inside is the best," Elena said. "Let's never go outside again."

The theater filled up, and everyone was loud and excited. Elena got a large popcorn and a small pop, and she went to the bathroom twice in the hour before the show started. "If I have to pee during the movie, I'm using this cup."

"It's what you do best," Gabe said.

"I can't believe I made it!" she said. "I can't believe we're here. I can't believe there's a new Star Wars movie."

"I can't believe how much I want a shower," Gabe said.

Elena started doing her Star Wars dance again. It worked just as well in a chair.

When the lights went down, she squealed.

She'd made it. She'd camped out. And she hadn't given up. And now it was here. Now it was starting.

The opening crawl began. *Episode VII: The Force Awakens.*

Elena felt all the stress and tension—all the

adrenalin—of the last four days drain out of her body. She felt like she was sinking deep, deep into the warm, plush chair.

She'd made it. She was here. It was happening.

FRIDAY
18 DECEMBER 2015

Elena woke up with her head on Gabe's shoulder. In a puddle of spit. Someone was trying to climb over her. "Excuse me," the person said. *Why would anyone be leaving during the opening credits?*

The opening credits. There were no opening credits.

Elena looked at Gabe. His head had fallen to the side, and his mouth was open. She shook his arm. *Violently.* "Gabe, Gabe, Gabe. Wake up! Gabe!"

He sat up like he'd been hit by lightning. "What?"

"We fell asleep," Elena said. "We fell asleep!"

"What?" He looked at the screen—"Oh my God!"—then back at Elena. "When did you fall asleep?"

"Immediately," she said. "As soon as the lights went off. Oh my Gahhhhd."

"I saw the crawl," Gabe said. "And a ship, I think?"

"We missed the whole thing," Elena said. Her chin was trembling.

"We missed the whole thing," Gabe repeated.

"We waited for a week, and then we missed the whole thing." He rested his elbows on his knees and buried his face in his hands. His shoulders started shaking.

Elena laid her hand on him. On the wet spot she'd left on his sleeve. She took her hand back and wiped it on her jeans.

Gabe sat back in his seat with his hands still in his hair. He was laughing so hard he looked like he was in pain.

Elena stared at him, in shock.

And then she started giggling.

And then she started guffawing.

"Elena! Gabe!" Troy was moving with the crowd towards the door. "Was it everything?"

"I'm speechless!" Elena shouted.

Gabe just kept laughing. "We slept on the *street*," he sputtered out. "You peed in a *dumpster*!"

Elena laughed so hard, her stomach hurt.

There were moments in the laughing when she felt totally miserable and wanted to cry—*she missed the whole thing!*—but that just made her laugh harder.

"What do we do now?" Gabe said. "Hit the street? Camp out until the next showing?"

"I'm going *home*," Elena said. "I'm going to sleep for twelve hours."

"Good idea," he said, sobering up a little. "Me, too."

Elena looked at him. At his curly brown hair and red stubble. She wondered what he'd look like when he hadn't been sleeping rough for a few days. (She'd know this if she ever picked up her head at school.) "We could come back tonight," she said. "We might be able to get tickets."

"I actually already have tickets," Gabe said, running his fingers through his hair. "I was going to come back at seven and see it again."

"Oh," Elena said. "Cool."

"You can have one . . ."

"I don't want to take someone else's ticket."

"It was for my cousin, and he can wait a day," Gabe said. "You've been waiting a week."

"I've been waiting my whole life," she said.

Gabe smiled at her.

Elena smiled back.

"Meet you tonight?" he said.

Elena nodded. "First person here gets in line."

Turn the page for an extract from . . .

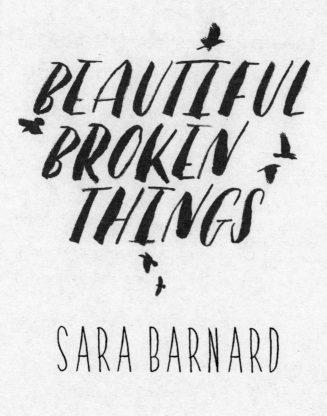

BEAUTIFUL
BROKEN
THINGS

SARA BARNARD

Before

I thought it was the start to a love story.

Finally.

The boy, who looked to be around my age or slightly older, had skidded to a stop in front of me. He gave me a quick, obvious once-over and then switched on a wide, flirtatious grin. His friend, better looking but very much not grinning flirtatiously at me, rolled his eyes.

'Heeeey,' the boy said, just like that. Heeeey.

'Hi,' I said, sending up a quick prayer that my bus wouldn't arrive before the conversation ended. I tried to flick my hair casually – difficult to do when it's a touch on the bushy side – and lifted my chin, like my sister once showed me when she was trying to teach me how to act confident.

'What flavour have you got?'

'What?'

He gestured to the ShakeAway cup in my hand. 'Oh,' I said, stupidly. 'Toblerone.' I'd only had a few sips of the milkshake. I liked to let it melt a little before I started drinking it properly, and the cup was heavy in my hand.

'Nice.' The boy carried on grinning at me. 'I've never tried that one. Can I have a sip?'

Here is what I was thinking as I handed over my milkshake: He likes ShakeAways! *I* like ShakeAways! This is a MOMENT. This is the START.

And then his back was to me and he and his friend were running away, their laughter lingering after them. When they were a few feet away, the boy turned, waving my cup triumphantly at me. 'Thanks, love!' he bellowed, either not realizing or not caring that he was not old enough – not to mention suave enough – to pull off 'love'.

I just stood there with my hand holding nothing but air. The other people at the bus stop were all staring at me, some hiding smirks, others clearly pained with second-hand embarrassment. I adjusted my bag strap as nonchalantly as I could, avoiding anyone's gaze, seriously considering stepping in front of a passing bus.

Three days ago I had turned sixteen – the first of my friends to hit this particular milestone, thanks to my early-September birthday – and my parents had rented out a hall for my birthday party. 'You can invite boys!' my mother had told me, looking more excited by this prospect than anyone. The problem wasn't that I didn't want boys (definitely not), the problem was that I went to a girls' school, and I could count the number of boys I knew well enough to speak to on one hand. Despite the efforts of my best friend, Rosie, who went to the mixed comprehensive and had plenty of boy/friends, the gender mix at the party was hopelessly unbalanced. I spent most of the night eating cake and talking with my friends rather than flirting wildly and dancing with what Rosie called potentials, like sixteen-year-olds are supposed to do. It wasn't a bad way to see in a new age, but it wasn't exactly spectacular either.

I mention this so my OK-have-my-milkshake-stranger idiocy has some context. I was sixteen, and I honestly believed that I was due a love story. Nothing epic (I'm not greedy), but something worth talking about. Someone to hold hands with (etc.). The milkshake meet-cute should have led to that. But instead I was just me, standing empty-handed, and the boy was just a boy.

When the bus pulled up just a couple of minutes later and I retreated to the anonymity of the top deck, I made a mental list of milestones I *would* have reached by the time my next birthday rolled around.

1) I would get a boyfriend. A real one.
2) I would lose my virginity.
3) I would experience a Significant Life Event.

In the following year I achieved just one of these goals. And it wasn't the one I expected.

'So he just *took* your milkshake?' Rosie's voice was sceptical. It was nearly 9 p.m., and she'd called me for our traditional last-night-before-school-starts chat.

'Yeah. Right out of my hand.'

'He just snatched it?'

'Um. Yes?'

There was a pause, followed by the sound of Rosie's laughter tickling down the line. Aside from my grandparents, Rosie was the only person I spoke to using the landline. 'Oh my God, Caddy, did you *give* it to him?'

'Not deliberately,' I said, already wishing I hadn't brought up the milkshake story. But it was always hard to stop myself telling Rosie everything. It was just second nature.

'I wish I'd been there.'

'Me too – you could have chased after him for me.'

Rosie and I had spent the day together, another before-school-starts tradition, and had actually bought a milkshake each before going our separate ways. She would definitely have chased after him, had she been there. When we were four, not long after we'd first met at a ballet class we both hated, an older boy had snatched my bow (I was the kind of kid who wore bows in her hair) and Rosie had sprinted after him, taken back the bow and stamped on his foot. Our friendship had followed a similar pattern ever since.

'Why didn't *you* chase him?'

'I was surprised!'

'You'd think after all this time in separate schools you'd have learned to chase your own bullies,' Rosie said, her voice light and teasing.

'Maybe Year 11 will be the year.'

'Maybe. Do they even have bullies in private school?'

'Yes.' She knew very well that they did. She was the one I'd cried to for several straight months in Year 8 when I'd been the target. My school, Esther Herring's High School for Girls, had more than its fair share of bullies.

'Oh yeah. Sorry. I mean boy bullies. Obviously you don't get those at Esther's. Those are the ones I chase for you.'

I let her tease me about teenage boy thieves for a few minutes more until we hung up. I headed back upstairs in the direction of my bedroom, walking past my mother, who was ironing in front of the TV.

'I've got your uniform here,' she called after me. 'Do you want to come and get it?'

I trudged reluctantly back towards her. My uniform was hanging on the cupboard door, the pleats on the skirt perfect, the blazer practically shining. I'd avoided looking at my uniform all summer. It was even greener than I remembered.

'All freshly ironed,' Mum said, looking pleased and proud. No one was happier that I was at Esther's than her. When she found out I'd got in, she cried. Actually we both cried, but mine were not happy tears.

'Thanks,' I said, taking the hangers.

'Are you excited about tomorrow?' She was smiling, and I wondered if she was being oblivious on purpose.

'Not really,' I said, but I injected a note of humour into my voice, to avoid a long 'don't disparage your opportunities' speech.

'It's a big year,' Mum said. The iron made a loud, squelching hissing noise, and she lifted it up. I suddenly realized she was ironing my father's pants.

'Mmmm,' I said, edging towards the door.

'It'll be a great one,' Mum continued happily, not even looking at me. 'I can already tell. Maybe they'll make you a prefect.'

This was unlikely. Being well behaved and getting good grades was not enough to set you apart at Esther's. The two prefects likely to be selected from my form were Tanisha, who'd started a feminist society in Year 9 and wanted to be prime minister, and Violet, who headed up the debating team and had campaigned successfully to get the school to go Fairtrade. Esther's was made for people like Tanisha and Violet. They didn't just achieve, which was expected to be a given for everyone, they thrived.

'Maybe,' I said. 'Don't be disappointed if I'm not though, OK?'

'I'll be disappointed at them, not you,' Mum replied, like this was any better.

Great, I thought. Another thing to worry about.

'I really hope you'll be focusing on your goals this year,' Mum said, looking up at me just as I tried to make my escape from the room. She was always big on goals.

I thought of the milestone list I'd mentally penned earlier on the bus. Boyfriend. Virginity. Significant Life Events.

'I am,' I said. 'Completely focused. Goodnight.'

Here's my theory on Significant Life Events: everyone has them, but some have more than others, and how many you have affects how interesting you are, how many stories you have to tell, that kind of thing. I was still waiting for my first one.

Not that I'm complaining, but my life up to the age of sixteen had been steady and unblemished. My parents were still married, my best friend had been constant for over ten years, I'd never been seriously ill and no one close to me had died. I'd also never won any major competition, been spotted for a talent (not that I had a talent) or really achieved anything beyond schoolwork.

This wasn't to say I hadn't been on the fringe of these kinds of events for other people. Rosie herself had had two, both bad. At two and a half her father walked out on her and her mother, never to be seen again. When she was eleven, her new baby sister, Tansy, was a cot-death victim. My older sister, Tarin, had been diagnosed with bipolar disorder at the age of eighteen, when I was ten, and the entire period of her diagnosis had been marked by dark clouds and tears and Serious Discussions. I'd experienced these latter two events from the middle of the storm, and had seen how they'd shaped the lives of two of my favourite people in the world.

Rosie and Tarin both thought my significant-life-event theory was ridiculous.

'Don't wish tragedy on yourself,' Tarin said. 'Or mental illness.' She didn't get it when I tried to explain that significant life events could be happy things as well. 'Like what?'

'Like getting married?' When her eyes went wide I added quickly, 'I mean in general, obviously, not for me any time soon.'

'God, Caddy, I hope you dream bigger than marriage as your life's significant event.'

Rosie was dismissive. 'They're just horrible things that happened, Cads. They don't make me more interesting than you.'

But the thing was, they did. The only interesting story I had to tell about my own life was that of my birth, which aside from my starring role as The Baby really had nothing to do with me. My parents, holidaying in Hampshire several weeks before my estimated arrival day, were stuck in a traffic jam in a little village called Cadnam when Mum went into labour. She ended up having me on the side of the road, with the help of a nurse who happened to be in another car.

This made a great story to pull out of the hat if I ever needed to, and I'd told it so many times ('Caddy's an interesting/weird/funny name. What's it short for?') I knew what kind of facial expressions to expect from the listener and the jokes they'd likely make ('Good thing they weren't driving through Croydon/Horsham/Slough! Ha!'). But that still didn't make it *mine*. I couldn't remember it, and it had no effect on my life. It was a significant event for my parents, not for me.

If anyone asked me for a story from my life in the present tense, I always went blank.

Of course I wasn't trying to invite tragedy into my life. I knew the takeaway from pain is sadness, not anecdotes. But everything about me and my life felt ordinary, hopelessly average, even clichéd. All I wanted was something of some significance to happen.

And then, so slowly at first I almost didn't notice it happening, it did.

2

Tuesday

Rosie, 09.07: New girl alert.

Caddy, 10.32: ??

10.34: We have a new girl!

10.39: Really? Details please.

**10.44: Her names Suzanne. Seems very cool.
More later, maths now.**

**13.19: She just moved here from Reading.
Takes same options as me! V funny.**

**13.20: I mean shes v funny, not the options
thing.**

13.28: Cool. How's everything else?

13.33: Same as. Call me tonight for chattage x

13.35: Will do x

Wednesday

**08.33: I am on the bus and I just realized I
forgot to brush my teeth.**

08.37: Lovely!

10.38: Guess who isn't a prefect?

10.40: Is it you?

10.42: Yes.

10.43: WOOOHOOOOOO! *streamers*

10.44: Your support means the world to me.

13.01: You will always be PREFECT to me!

13.05: Um, thanks?

13.06: Geddit?

13.09: Yes!

13.11: HAHAHAHAHA. Suzanne says I shouldn't laugh because maybe you wanted to be prefect.

13.29: You told her?

13.33: Yeah! I told her you def didnt want to be prefect and I'm laughing in a good way.

13.35: Sz says all of the best people she knows aren't prefects.

13.40: Cads?

13.46: I def didn't want to be prefect. Mum wanted me to be though.

13.48: :(

13.49: We'll be not prefects together xx

<u>Thursday</u>

13.19: Nikki has clocked that Suzanne is cool. She tried to get her to sit with her at lunch.

13.25: Successfully?

13.27: No. Suzanne said she was good with me. Nikki said, you must have noticed she's a loser by now. Sz was like, wtf? and Nikki goes 'SERIOUSLY. I'm SAVING YOU.'

13.28: Bitch!!! Are you OK?

13.29. No. I'm crying in the toilets.

13.30: Want me to call you?

13.31: No.

13.31: Yes please.

<u>Friday</u>

09.01: What did you have for breakfast this morning?

09.02: Um, cereal?

09.03: Mum made me pancakes. I WIN!

13.12: Idea. How about I bring Suzanne with me when I come to yours after school? Then you can meet her!

13.42: Sure, OK.

13.43: Yay! You'll love her, she's amazing. We'll come straight over, probs be at yours at about 4.

13.58: See you then x

15.33: WEEKEND!!!

BEAUTIFUL BROKEN THINGS

I was brave
She was reckless
We were trouble

Best friends Caddy and Rosie are inseparable. Their differences have brought them closer, but as she turns sixteen Caddy begins to wish she could be a bit more like Rosie: confident, funny and interesting. Then Suzanne comes into their lives – beautiful, damaged, exciting and mysterious – and things get a whole lot more complicated. As Suzanne's past is revealed and her present begins to unravel, Caddy begins to see how much fun a little trouble can be. But the course of both friendship and recovery is rougher than either girl realizes, and Caddy is about to learn that downward spirals have a momentum of their own.

Find out more at www.mykindabook.com/ books/beautiful-broken-things

WORLD BOOK DAY fest

Want to READ more?

SPONSORED BY
NATIONAL
BOOK
tokens

VISIT **YOUR LOCAL BOOKSHOP**

- Get some great recommendations for what to read next
- Meet your favourite authors & illustrators at brilliant events
- Discover books you never even knew existed!

FIND YOUR LOCAL BOOKSHOP   www.booksellers.org.uk/bookshopsearch

JOIN **YOUR LOCAL LIBRARY**

You can browse and borrow from a HUGE selection of books and get recommendations of what to read next from expert librarians—all for **FREE**! You can also discover libraries' wonderful children's and family reading activities.

FIND YOUR LOCAL LIBRARY   www.findalibrary.co.uk

GET ONLINE

VISIT **WORLDBOOKDAY.COM** TO DISCOVER A WHOLE NEW WORLD OF BOOKS!

- Downloads and activities for top books and authors
- Cool games, trailers and videos
- Author events in your area
- News, competitions and new books—all in a FREE monthly email

AND MORE!

Instant
TIME
MANAGEMENT